Happy Squirrels

 Can you spot 3 differences between the pictures below?

Things That Move!

✏️ Match the vehicles with their modes of transportation.

Match the Shadows

✏️ Match the animals with their shadows.

Rabbit Maze

✏ Help the rabbit reach the carrots.

Let's Count

Observe the picture and answer the questions.

How many rabbits?

How many clouds?

How many flowers?

Not Quite Right!

✏ Each mouse is missing something. Draw the missing part.

Odd One Out

Observe the emotions and choose the odd one out.

Let's Go!

✏ Help the hedgehog pick all the apples in a basket and reach the tree.

Find and Circle

✏️ Find and circle the objects given below.

Spot the Differences

✏️ Find 5 differences in the pictures given below.

Answer

Fun Picnic

Count these objects and write the answers in the boxes given below.

Healthy Eating

✏️ Crossout the unhealthy food items.

How Would You Feel?

✏ Circle the face you would make in these situations.

What's my Sound?

✏ Circle the animal that makes the sound given on the left.

Oink Oink			
Meow			
Neigh			
Moo			
Woof Woof			

Expressive Dogs

Circle the dog that exactly matches the one on the left.

Strawberry Hunt

Find and count all the strawberries in the image. Write down the total in the box given above.